Olive A. Wadsworth

Over in the Meadow

A Counting-Out Rhyme

Pictures by
Mary Maki Rae

VIKING KESTREL

*For the flora and fauna
on the following pages,
And children of all ages.*

M.M.R.

VIKING KESTREL

Viking Penguin Inc., 40 West 23rd Street, New York, New York 10010, U.S.A.
Penguin Books Ltd, Harmondsworth, Middlesex, England
Penguin Books Australia Ltd, Ringwood, Victoria, Australia
Penguin Books Canada Limited, 2801 John Street, Markham, Ontario, Canada L3R 1B4
Penguin Books (N.Z.) Ltd, 182–190 Wairau Road, Auckland 10, New Zealand

Illustrations copyright © Mary Maki Rae, 1985   All rights reserved
First published in 1985 by Viking Penguin Inc.   Published simultaneously in Canada

Library of Congress Cataloging in Publication Data
Wadsworth, Olive A.   Over in the meadow.
Summary: Rhymed verses about different animals living
in a meadow introduce the numbers one through ten.
1. Children's stories, American.   [1. Stories in rhyme.
2. Animals—Fiction.   3. Counting]   I. Rae, Mary Maki, ill.   II. Title.
PZ8.3.W132Ov   1985   [E]   84-19653   ISBN 0-670-53276-2

Printed in Japan by Dai Nippon   1   2   3   4   5   89   88   87   86   85
Set in Cheltenham Book

Over in the meadow in the sand in the sun
Lived an old mother turtle and her little turtle one.
Dig, said the mother. *We dig*, said the one.
So they dug all day in the sand in the sun.

Over in the meadow where the stream runs blue
Lived an old mother fish and her little fishes two.
Swim, said the mother. *We swim,* said the two.
So they swam all day where the stream runs blue.

Over in the meadow in a hole in a tree
Lived an old mother owl and her little owls three.
Tu-whoo, said the mother. *Tu-whoo*, said the three.
So they tu-whooed all day in a hole in a tree.

Over in the meadow by the old barn door
Lived an old mother rat and her little ratties four.
Gnaw, said the mother. *We gnaw*, said the four.
So they gnawed all day by the old barn door.

Over in the meadow in a snug beehive
Lived an old mother bee and her little bees five.
Buzz, said the mother.
We buzz, said the five.
So they buzzed all day
in a snug beehive.

Over in the meadow in a nest built of sticks
Lived an old mother crow and her little crows six.
Caw, said the mother. *We caw,* said the six.
So they cawed all day in a nest built of sticks.

Over in the meadow where the grass grows so even
Lived an old mother frog and her little froggies seven.
Jump, said the mother. *We jump*, said the seven.
So they jumped all day where the grass grows so even.

Over in the meadow by the old mossy gate
Lived an old mother lizard and her little lizards eight.
Bask, said the mother. *We bask*, said the eight.
So they basked all day by the old mossy gate.

Over in the meadow by the old Scotch pine
Lived an old mother duck and her little ducks nine.
Quack, said the mother.
We quack, said the nine.
So they quacked all day
by the old Scotch pine.

Over in the meadow in a cozy wee den
Lived an old mother beaver and her little beavers ten.
Beave, said the mother.   *We beave,* said the ten.
So they beaved all day in a cozy wee den.

1 2

5

7 8